Scooby-Doo
Pirates Ahoy

Scooby-Doo
Pirates Ahoy

SCHOLASTIC INC.

New York   Toronto   London   Auckland   Sydney
Mexico City   New Delhi   Hong Kong   Buenos Aires

No part of this publication may be reproduced in whole or in part, or stored in a retrieval system, or transmitted in any form or by any means, electronic, mechanical, photocopying, recording, or otherwise, without written permission of the publisher. For information regarding permission, write to Scholastic Inc., Attention: Permissions Department, 557 Broadway, New York, NY 10012.

ISBN 0-439-83992-0

Designed by Michael Massen

12 11 10 9 8 7 6 5 4 3 2 1   5 6 7 8 9/0

Printed in the U.S.A.
First printing, October 2006

Scooby-Doo Pirates Ahoy

Introduction

Dr. Rupert Garcia stood on the deck of a ship named the *Galaxy Gazer*. She was sailing in the calm waters of the infamous Bermuda Triangle. "This place gives me the creeps," said one of the deckhands who was mopping the deck nearby.

Rupert chuckled. He knew all the scary old stories about the Bermuda Triangle. "Vanishing ships . . . sea monsters . . . aliens," he said. "They're all just legends. Don't let them scare you."

After a while, Rupert went to his cabin, which was filled with everything he needed for his work as an astrologer: telescopes, drafting tables, star charts, and computer screens of various sizes. He stopped a moment to look at a painting that hung on the wall. It was a two-hundred-year-old painting of a shooting star falling into the ocean in the Bermuda Triangle. It was one of a kind and it was his most treasured possession.

Rupert got back to work on his star map at his drawing table. He was working so intently that he didn't notice a spooky fog rolling in outside his porthole window.

He looked up, though, when he heard an eerie whistling. The sound grew louder . . . LOUDER . . .

BAM!

The cabin lurched forward violently, sending Rupert flying. The *Galaxy Gazer* had been struck by something!

Rupert peered out the porthole. He saw an old pirate ship appear out of the fog. As it turned, Rupert could see that the cannon on the pirate ship's deck was aimed right at the the *Galaxy Gazer*!

"What the heck?" he cried.

BAM! The cabin lurched as it was struck by a cannonball fired from the pirate ship!

The blast knocked Rupert off his feet! He slid across the tilting floor. He hit his head hard against one of the legs of his worktable and lay there under it, barely conscious.

Water seeped in from under the door.

Could it be? Were they . . . sinking?

The door to Rupert's cabin flew open. *BANG!*

Peeking out from under the table, Rupert saw two men — they were dressed like pirates!

Pirates?

Was he was seeing things? No, he wasn't! One of the pirates was tall and strong. The other was smaller and one of his legs was made of wood.

The pirates threw Rupert's things all around, searching for something. They tossed his star map to the floor. They hurled his drawing tools across the cabin. "Here it is, Cap'n Skunkbeard," cried the one with the wooden leg.

"Ah, good work, Wooden Leg Wally," Captain Skunkbeard praised him. "Now, where is *he*?"

"Maybe he's with the rest of the crew," Wooden Leg Wally suggested.

"Blimey!" the captain shouted angrily. "Board all hands below in the bilge and we'll sort them all out later."

The two pirates stomped out of the cabin. As soon as they were gone, Rupert got up and staggered across the cabin and out onto the deck. He looked out into the foggy night. Below him in the water he saw a long, open boat rowed by pirates. It carried the entire crew of the *Galaxy Gazer* and was returning to the ghostly pirate ship! Rupert was the only one left on board! "This can't be happening!" he murmured.

BAM!

A second cannonball struck the *Galaxy Gazer*. The blast threw Rupert right over the ship's railing and into the black ocean waves below.

Chapter 1

The Mystery Machine turned into the Port of Miami. It passed rows of tall cruise ships, all docked side by side in their own piers.

When the van arrived at Pier 45, it stopped. Shaggy Rogers stuck his head out of the back door and smiled. "Finally, a trip where there are no monsters," he said, climbing out of the Mystery Machine. Lately, he and the gang had been busier than ever, solving one *scarifying* case after the other. He was ready for a rest.

Scooby-Doo, the Great Dane who was Shaggy's best pal, jumped out of the back door of the Mystery Machine. He crashed into a very short, very creepy-looking little man who was standing nearby.

"*Ri-i-i-kes!*" Scooby shouted. His ears rose into the air with fright and he leaped into Shaggy's arms as he always did when he was scared.

Shaggy looked all around, trying to see what had upset Scooby so much — but he didn't see anything. The creepy little man had vanished.

The rest of the gang rushed back from the front of the van. "What's going on, guys?" Fred asked when he saw Scooby-Doo shivering in Shaggy's arms.

"I don't know. Something spooked Scooby," Shaggy replied.

The gang were all suddenly blinded by the bright light of a flash camera.

"I hope you all packed your sea legs," said Skip Jones, Fred's father, lowering his camera.

"And a new set of eyeballs," Velma quipped, rubbing her eyes beneath her glasses.

It was Fred's birthday, and his parents had invited the whole gang on a cruise to celebrate!

"Pop!" Fred cried happily. Skip Jones looked like an older, rounder version of Fred. He was dressed in a bright Hawaiian-print shirt and Bermuda shorts. Fred and his dad did their secret handshake.

"Freddy! My baby!" Peggy Jones cried. Fred's mother was a pleasantly plump woman in a large beach hat, a flower-print dress, and oversize sunglasses. She grabbed Fred's cheeks and shook them lovingly. "Have you ever seen such a good-looking boy? Give me some sugar!"

Fred blushed until his face couldn't have gotten any redder. "Mom!" he complained.

Skip and Peggy led the gang up the long stairway to the cruise ship.

"Where exactly is this cruise ship headed, Mr. Jones?" Daphne asked as they climbed the stairs.

"That's a surprise. I've got the perfect birthday plan," Skip Jones replied.

The moment they were all on deck, a woman in a blue jacket and white skirt, and an even whiter smile, hurried over to them. "Welcome aboard the *Poseidon's Paradise*," she greeted them cheerily. "I'm Sunny St. Cloud, your cruise director."

Skip Jones flashed a photo that left Sunny St. Cloud rubbing her eyes.

"Well, aren't you the perky one," Peggy Jones said. "We're the Jones party."

Sunny St. Cloud led the gang to their cabins.

Shaggy and Scooby-Doo were at the back of the line as their friends followed Sunny St. Cloud below deck. They heard something behind them and turned around. What they saw terrified them.

"*AAHHH!*" Screaming, they jumped into the air!

It was the creepy little man — the same one who had frightened Scooby-Doo back on the pier!

Fred, Daphne, and Velma hurried over to see what was wrong. "Scooby was right!" Shaggy shouted. "I saw him, too — a little creepy dude with scary eyes."

"*Ruh-huh! Ruh-huh!*" Scooby-Doo agreed, nodding frantically.

"But there's no one creepy around here, Shaggy," Daphne pointed out. Just as she spoke, though, the creepy little man walked past them again.

"Except maybe that guy," Velma said in a low voice.

The little man turned into one of the rooms down the hall. As the gang watched him, Sunny St. Cloud stopped in front of one of the doors.

"Here are your cabins," she announced. "They are all right next door to one another. Your bags should already be inside."

"But what about the creepy guy?" Shaggy asked.

"No time for him now," Sunny said cheerily. "You have exactly ninety seconds to freshen up and then meet me on the upper deck."

Shaggy's face brightened into a wide grin. "No time for creeps — sounds good to me!"

Chapter 2

The gang unpacked and joined Fred's parents in the ship's navigation cabin, where the controls and the wheel that steered the boat were located. There they met the ship's captain. "Captain Crothers," Daphne said. "Where is this ship headed?"

"We are bound for one of the most mysterious places on Earth," replied Captain Crothers. "The Bermuda Triangle!"

Scooby-Doo and Shaggy moved closer to each other, their knees knocking together.

Velma was not impressed. "Oh, please," she scoffed. "The legend of the Bermuda Triangle is just that — a legend!"

"Trust me, after this cruise, you'll believe in the power of the Triangle," Captain Crothers warned. As he spoke, the lights in the cabin began to flicker. The dials on the control panel spun around wildly. A bright, white, blinding light flashed.

"Where did Captain Crothers go?" Velma cried out. The captain seemed to have disappeared!

"We're in the Bermuda Triangle and the captain has disappeared!" Shaggy whined in a high, panicked voice. "Abandon ship!"

"Look!" Daphne shouted, pointing out the window overlooking the main deck. A tall figure of an alien was passing across the deck just outside the window.

"Gang, it's trap-setting time!" Fred said excitedly.

Shaggy and Scooby rolled their eyes at one another. "Maaaan," Shaggy said with a moan. "You know what that means, buddy."

"Rive rait," Scooby-Doo said, nodding.

"That's right, pal," Shaggy agreed glumly. "As usual, I'm sure we'll be the live bait."

Less than an hour later, Scooby-Doo and Shaggy were on deck dressed like members of the ship's crew. Mops in their hands, they pretended to wash down the deck.

Daphne and Fred stood nearby. "You know what to do, right?" Fred checked.

"Go to the dining room, get something to eat, and forget the whole thing," Shaggy suggested hopefully.

Fred smiled but shook his head. "No."

"I didn't think that would work," Shaggy admitted. He and Scooby-Doo continued to mop as Daphne and Fred walked away. As they mopped, they moved along down the deck past a large, curved vent pipe. The sound of a slight cough made Shaggy and Scooby-Doo turn toward the vent.

The creepy little guy was inside, staring out at them with his wide, spooky eyes!

Scooby-Doo and Shaggy screamed and leaped in terror. Together they raced away from the creepy guy. With a screech of sliding feet, they rounded the corner of the deck and smacked straight into — the alien!

"Yikes!" shouted Shaggy as they knocked him to the ground.

Scooby-Doo and Shaggy turned and ran in the opposite direction. The alien got to its feet and chased after them.

It chased them upstairs and into the banquet room. The alien pursued them across a buffet table and through the ship's kitchen. It swam after them when they plunged into the pool, chasing them up the high diving board and back into the pool again.

Scooby-Doo and Shaggy were tired of running, but they didn't stop until the alien suddenly rose high into the air and hung upside down!

Fred's trap had worked!

The alien had stepped right into a noose on the ground and now hung by its foot from a rope attached to a pole. Peggy Jones stepped out from behind a stack of deck chairs and snapped a photo of the hanging alien. Sunny, Skip Jones, Daphne, Velma, and Fred quickly came out from hiding, too. "Impressive, son," Skip praised Fred proudly.

"Thanks, Pop," Fred replied happily.

"Well, I think I have this mystery all figured out," Velma announced.

"Really?" Shaggy questioned, impressed. "That was quick."

"*Reah*," Scooby-Doo agreed.

"I know who's under this mask," Velma insisted. She reached down, grabbed the top of the alien's head, and began to pull.

Chapter 3

"Captain Crothers!" The gang and the Joneses cried at once.

Captain Crothers shrugged and the gang realized that Sunny St. Cloud didn't seem very surprised. They stared at her, waiting for an explanation. "Well, it wouldn't be much of a Bermuda Triangle Mystery Cruise without an alien abduction, now, would it?" she said.

The gang gasped. "Mystery cruise?" they said together.

"Surprise!" Skip and Peggy Jones shouted happily.

"Ya, we know how much you kids love mysteries," Peggy Jones explained. "What better way to celebrate Fred's birthday?"

Fred smiled from ear to ear. "Wow! Thanks, Mom. Thanks, Pop!"

The next two days were jammed full of fake

mysteries for the gang to solve. The problem was, there was no mystery that Sunny St. Cloud, Captain Crothers, or the crew staged that the gang couldn't solve.

This made Sunny St. Cloud unhappy. "We've gone through a week's worth of mysteries in two days!" she complained on the second day at sea.

"Sorry," Daphne apologized. "Mysteries are kind of our thing."

Looking around, the gang realized that the other passengers on the ship were looking at them angrily. "What good is a mystery cruise if you don't get to solve any mysteries!" a man complained loudly.

"Sorry, everybody," Fred told them. "We didn't mean to ruin the cruise for you."

The Mystery, Inc. gang watched as the other passengers and Sunny St. Cloud stormed off. Captain Crothers approached them. "It's too bad for us that there doesn't seem to be any mystery that you can't solve," he said.

"Like, there's *one* thing I don't understand," Shaggy admitted. "What's with the weird cast-away out there?

Everyone ran to the side of the ship and looked down at the water to where Shaggy was pointing.

Rupert Garcia was floating there, weak, and clinging to a life preserver!

"Man overboard!" Captain Crothers shouted.

The ship's crane hoisted Rupert from the sea to safety. He landed on the ship's deck with a thud! His clothing was frayed and his beard was grizzled. It was clear that he'd been floating out there a long time.

The gang, Captain Crothers, and Peggy and Skip Jones huddled around. Rupert told them the story of how a ghostly pirate ship had attacked and sunk the *Galaxy Gazer* and stolen her crew.

Captain Crothers thought that Rupert had been driven mad from sun, hunger, and thirst. He insisted that he go belowdecks to see the ship's doctor.

The gang didn't believe Rupert's story, either. This had to be just another of the ship's put-on mysteries.

"Don't worry," Fred told Sunny St. Cloud. "We'll keep the 'Pirate Puzzler Mystery' for the other guests to solve."

Sunny looked at him, not seeming to understand. But before she could reply, the sound of a buzzing engine filled the air. A man strapped to a jet pack appeared above them. He waved as he flew overhead. "Ahoy, below!" he greeted them as he flew down toward the deck.

"That's Biff Wellington, the extremely odd but extremely rich billionaire!" Daphne said as the man landed nearby.

Biff Wellington smiled, unstrapping his jet pack. Velma stepped toward him. "Excuse me for asking, Mr. Wellington, but what are you doing out here in the middle of nowhere?"

"I'm setting the record for the first round-the-world jet pack flight," he explained, shrugging out of his pack. "And it seems that I've run out of gas. Can you spare some fuel, Captain?"

"Okay," Captain Crothers agreed. "Follow me."

As Biff Wellington walked off with the captain, Velma grinned and turned toward Sunny St. Cloud. "The eccentric billionaire with a jet pack is a nice touch, Sunny," she said.

"What do you mean?" Sunny asked.

"Don't worry," Daphne added. "We promise we won't get involved."

This was great news to Shaggy and Scooby-Doo!

"We're not getting involved in a mystery! Pinch me, Scoob, I must be dreaming!" Shaggy said with a smile.

Sunny St. Cloud's beeper sounded and she checked her watch. "Time to move, people," she told them. "Only fifteen minutes before the costume party, dinner, and a mystery show." She gazed at the gang meaningfully. "And try not to spoil it for the others."

Chapter 4

At the costume party, Fred dressed as Indiana Jones. Daphne came as Catwoman, and Velma dressed up as a scientist. When Scooby-Doo and Shaggy entered the ship's party room, the gang laughed. They had put on a two-headed chicken costume.

Fred was surprised to see his dad dressed as a castaway. He looked just the same as Rupert Garcia had looked when they fished him out of the ocean, only Skip Jones had added a wig and fake beard. "Pop, are you wearing Rupert's old clothes?" he asked.

Skip Jones nodded proudly. "Can't get a more real-looking castaway costume than this, now, can you?"

Mrs. Jones came up beside him, dressed as a native of a tropical island, in a wraparound, strapless dress with a hat made of fruit on her head. She pinched her husband playfully. "You look so adorable, hon," she said with a giggle. "I'd rescue you any time."

Rupert Garcia joined them. Skip Jones had given him a clean pair of shorts and one of his Hawaiian shirts. He'd washed and shaved. "You're looking better," Daphne said to him.

"Yes, thanks to Skip, I feel like myself before the ghost —"

"Okay, okay, enough of that silly pirate talk," Mrs. Jones cut him off. Like everyone else, she thought Rupert had imagined the pirate ghost ship and it would be best if he just forgot about it. "Let's find our table and eat."

The gang, Rupert, and the Joneses seated themselves at a round table, and waiters began to serve them. Sunny St. Cloud came by and admired their costumes.

She checked her watch and smiled. "It's time for the show!" she told everyone.

The room got dark, and spooky music played. In a spotlight in the center of the stage, the creepy little dude Shaggy and Scooby had been seeing all around appeared. "I am Mr. Mysterio," he announced. "There is no one I can not hypnotize." He stared at Scooby-Doo and Shaggy with his wide eyes.

Mr. Mysterio was almost right. With the exception of Scooby, Shaggy, Fred, Daphne, Velma, Skip, and Rupert, soon the whole audience was in a trance.

Suddenly all the lights went out. An eerie fog gathered in the porthole windows.

"Oh, no!" Rupert whispered. "It's happening again!" He hurried to the window, followed by the gang and the Joneses.

A bloodcurdling laugh filled the ship's dark ballroom.

"I know I'm not going to like the answer, but I'll ask, anyway," Shaggy said in a shaky voice. "What was that?"

"Ghost pirates," Rupert replied.

"*Zoinks!*" Shaggy whimpered. "I knew I wouldn't like it!"

A ghostly face appeared in the porthole, his green eyes burning in the darkness. It was the ghost of Captain Skunkbeard!

"Gee, Captain Crothers, that ghost pirate sure is realistic-looking," Fred said, certain that this was just another of the ship's set-up mysteries.

Shaggy tapped Fred on the shoulder and pointed across the ballroom. Together, the gang turned. In the darkness, they could just make out the outline of the captain — and he was trembling in fear like everyone else.

"Jinkies, Rupert, you were right," Velma said.

Suddenly, the wall to the party room came crashing down. Splinters flew everywhere and the eerie fog rolled in. Captain Skunkbeard and Wooden Leg Wally entered. "Who dares sail into the Bermuda Triangle?" Captain Skunkbeard shouted. "Ye have crossed paths with Captain Skunkbeard the pirate, and ye shall pay the price." Captain Skunkbeard's green eyes searched the crowd.

Rupert clutched Fred's arm fearfully. He worried that the pirate was looking for him, and the next words Captain Skunkbeard spoke made him certain. "I know ye be here, ye scurvy coward. Ye escaped me once, but not a second time will ye hide from the fury of Captain Skunkbeard!"

The gang looked out the window and saw the ghostly pirate ship come alongside the

Fred's parents were taking the whole Mystery, Inc. gang on a cruise to the mysterious Bermuda Triangle.

In the ship's nightclub, Mr. Mysterio performed his act. He hypnotized everyone in the audience, except for Shaggy and Scooby!

Meanwhile, the rest of the gang, along with Fred's dad and Rupert, went on deck to check out the mysterious ghost pirate ship.

The ghost pirates, led by Captain Skunkbeard and Woodenleg Wally, captured the gang and all the other passengers, and sank the cruise ship!

According to the star map, Captain Skunkbeard was almost at the center of the Bermuda Triangle!

The phantoms of the Bermuda Triangle paid a visit to the ghost pirate ship.

The gang snuck free and found a secret room. They found models that looked like the Bermuda Triangle phantoms, and a projector.

Meanwhile, Captain Skunkbeard found what he had been searching for: the Heaven's Light meteor. "Now the power of the Bermuda Triangle will be mine!" he cried.

The gang set a trap. Captain Skunkbeard was really billionaire Biff Wellington! He thought that the meteor would let him travel through time and control the seas!

The crazy idea had come from Woodenleg Wally. He was really Mr. Mysterio! And the meteor was solid gold! "I'll be richer than you, Wellington," Mr. Mysterio boasted.

Mr. Mysterio had created the phantoms of the Triangle to convince Wellington to look for the meteor, and had hypnotized the passengers on the cruise ship to act like ghost pirates.

The gang returned the meteor to the sea, and Mr. Mysterio un-hypnotized the passengers. Captain Scooby steered the pirate ship back home. "Ro-ho-ho and Scooby-Dooby-Doo!"

cruise ship. Ghost pirates were boarding. "We have to get out of here!" Rupert cried.

The ghost pirates swarmed into the dark room. Screaming passengers tried to flee. In the fog and the darkness it was hard to see anything.

Soon, Fred realized that he hadn't seen his parents in a while. He searched for them frantically in the confusion. By the time the room became quiet again, he still hadn't found them.

He looked out the porthole window and saw the ghost ship sailing away. It had taken all the passengers on the cruise ship except for the gang. Fred saw his parents standing on the deck of the ghost ship with the others. All prisoners of Captain Skunkbeard!

The gang raced to the empty navigation cabin where they had first met Captain Crothers. Fred stood behind the ship's big wheel. Daphne and Velma took the other controls while Rupert studied his star maps. Shaggy and Scooby went to the front of the boat to keep a lookout for the pirate ship. Soon they caught sight of the ghostly pirates dead ahead of them. They seemed to be having a big party!

When Scooby and Shaggy gave the signal, Fred steered the ship at full speed right for the pirates.

"Freddie, so what's our plan?" Velma asked, sure that Fred would have one of his big plans ready to go.

"I'm going to ram them!" Fred replied.

Chapter 5

Meanwhile, on the pirate ship, the ghost pirates were having a great time. They were happy over their big capture of the cruise ship and its passengers. Captain Skunkbeard spoke to his men as they partied on the upper deck of their ship. "Tonight, me hearties, we are on the verge of greatness. When the tide is nigh, we will unleash the power of the Heaven's Light! We will open the portal to times past and we will once again travel the seas of yore!"

The pirates cheered although they really had no idea what Captain Skunkbeard was talking about. They didn't notice that Skip Jones, still dressed in the castaway costume he'd borrowed from Rupert, had come up on deck and was also listening to Captain Skunkbeard's wild words.

"We will regain our lost treasures and reign supreme over the seas," the captain went on, speaking even louder to be heard above the pirates' cheers and shouts of "Yo! Ho!" He suddenly stopped talking. He'd noticed Skip Jones standing there and pointed to him. Everyone turned and stared at Fred's father. "This scurvy dog can lead us to the location of the Heaven's Light. He alone holds the key to our destiny!"

"I keep telling you, I don't know anything about stars or maps!" Skip Jones cried. Ever since he was captured, the pirates had been asking Skip Jones about star maps. They obviously thought he was Rupert since he was wearing Rupert's clothing. No matter how much Skip tried to tell the pirates he knew nothing about star maps, they wouldn't believe him.

A short, plump female pirate stepped forward, a huge pirate sword at her waist. "Make him walk the plank!" she shouted.

"Aye! Now there's an idea!" Captain Skunkbeard shouted excitedly. "Matey, who be ye that brings forth such a brilliant and pirate suggestion."

"It be I, Cap'n, Sea Salt Sally!" the female pirate replied.

"Oh, Scooby-Doo, where are you?" Skip Jones muttered, his knees trembling.

The pirate keeping watch up in the ship's crow's nest suddenly shouted down a warning. "Ship ho! In chase at a timely clip!"

Skip Jones smiled quietly. "It's Freddy," he said to himself.

Captain Skunkbeard ordered his pirates to their battle stations. He ran to the ship's cannon and launched a cannonball directly at the approaching cruise ship. He cheered as it hit the cruise ship's bow, blowing a hole right in its side. They fired again and again!

The cruise ship carrying Rupert Garcia, Scooby-Doo, and the rest of the gang began breaking apart. Large chunks of it were falling into the ocean. It was about to sink!

Wooden Leg Wally and the rest of the pirates joined Captain Skunkbeard's cheer. They watched as the cruise ship disappeared beneath the waves.

"Freddy!" Skip Jones sobbed, watching the ship go under.

In the excitement, the pirates had almost

forgotten about Skip Jones. But, now, everyone turned toward him.

Captain Skunkbeard waved his sword at the plump female pirate. "You, Sea Salt Sally, get him ready to walk the plank!" he ordered.

Sea Salt Sally beckoned for two pirates to help her carry Skip Jones away. "Tell me what you've done with my wife!" he demanded as he struggled to free himself from the pirates' grasp.

Sea Salt Sally tied a bandanna around his mouth and laughed. "Whoever that poor woman is — she'll be thanking me for this," she said.

Chapter 6

Scooby-Doo, the gang, and Rupert crawled wearily onto the sandy shore of a small tropical island. They set out to search the island and soon discovered some very modern-looking stairs running down the side of a steep cliff.

Scooby-Doo leaned against the side of the cliff, bumping into a large stone. The stone began to rumble and then swung open, revealing a huge cave! "Where's the light switch?" Shaggy asked.

"This cave is hundreds of years old," Velma told him. "There is certainly no —" She stopped talking abruptly as the cave was suddenly bathed in light. "— light switch." She finished her sentence in a small voice as, one after another, rows and rows of lights lit up. "I stand corrected," she added.

"My boat!" Rupert shouted joyfully. The *Galaxy Gazer* floated in a shallow pool just ahead of them. Rupert ran to it with the gang right behind him. When they got closer to the boat, they saw that the shallow pool was connected to a narrow stream.

They all climbed aboard the *Galaxy Gazer*, standing on its top deck.

"The ghost pirates must have brought the *Galaxy Gazer* back to this cave for some reason," Daphne said.

Rupert went into his cabin and came back out a moment later looking pale. "My antique painting is gone," he said. "It was a painting of the night sky over the Bermuda Triangle, done two hundred years ago."

"What would the ghost pirates want with an old painting of stars?" Velma wondered aloud.

"Why don't you ask them?" Shaggy suggested, his voice trembling.

They all turned and faced Captain Skunkbeard and Wooden Leg Wally standing in front of a group of their ghost pirates. "Looks like we have some uninvited guests to our secret lair,"

Captain Skunkbeard said, his voice booming. "Prepare to suffer the wrath of Captain Skunkbeard!"

The gang sat, tied to the mast of Captain Skunkbeard's ghostly ship. "Pop!" Fred cried as his father came up from belowdecks with his hands tied behind his back, pushed along by Sea Salt Sally. "Where's Mom?" he asked.

"Stow, ye scurvy pup!" Sea Salt Sally snapped at him angrily.

"My painting!" Rupert cried. His painting was leaning on the ship near Captain Skunkbeard.

The captain looked sharply over to Rupert and then to Skip Jones. "Methinks we have the wrong man," he said, realizing his mistake. He pointed his sword at Rupert. "This is the man who will lead me to what I seek!"

Roughly, Captain Skunkbeard cut Rupert free and dragged him to his feet. Then he ordered his pirates to tie Skip Jones to the mast along with the others.

"The stars in the painting must be some kind of map," Velma figured, whispering to her friends.

"But a map to where?" Fred asked, whispering back.

As they spoke, an eerie light began to glow in the sky. Suddenly, they heard the whirring sound of a plane propeller, and five old-fashioned World War I fighter planes appeared in the sky.

"Aye, the Phantoms of the Triangle!" Captain Skunkbeard shouted. "All the ghostly vessels that have been lost in the Bermuda Triangle are appearing to try to frighten us off. We must be getting close!"

The gang and Skip Jones saw another ship coming alongside the ghost ship. The name *Cyclops* was written on its well-worn hull. "The *Cyclops*!" Velma exclaimed. "That ship's been missing for more than a hundred years!"

A surge of water swept the deck as a giant sea monster raised its head from the ocean's depths! It's huge dragonlike tail slapped the waves.

"We must be going into the heart of the Bermuda Triangle!" Fred guessed.

"Be hearty, me mates," Captain Skunkbeard shouted to his crew. "This is our moment of truth!"

While the pirates were gaping at the strange things going on around them, Daphne used her fingernails to work a small makeup bag free from her pocket. Using a nail file, she quietly sawed through her ropes. In minutes she was free and began untying the others. "We have to find the other captives," Fred whispered to his dad. "Do you know where they are, Pop?"

"Ah, jeez," Skip Jones replied in a whisper, "I haven't seen anyone else but the ghost pirates."

"They must be belowdecks," Velma suggested.

"This way," Fred said, sneaking quietly in the direction of the lower deck. Silently, Skip Jones and the gang followed him. On the lower deck, they hid behind a row of barrels and watched as Captain Skunkbeard, Wooden Leg Wally, and the other pirates crowded around a table where Rupert sat looking down at his painting.

"We're almost there," Rupert told the pirates. He was pointing to a spot where a shooting star seemed to be falling into the ocean. "But there's nothing out here but hundreds of miles of open sea."

"Land ho!" a pirate called from his lookout perch in the crow's nest. From behind their barrels, the gang and Skip Jones were astonished. Rupert had just said there was nothing around here. Had he been lying? It didn't seem so, because he also looked amazed.

Captain Skunkbeard grinned as he took an old map from his coat pocket. In the middle of it was a ring of rocks surrounding a volcano. "At the center we will find the Heaven's Light which fell to Earth centuries ago."

Rupert glanced at his painting and suddenly realized what Captain Skunkbeard was talking about. "Do you mean a meteor?" he asked.

Captain Skunkbeard nodded. "The Heaven's Light is the source of the Triangle's amazing power. After tonight, the power will be mine. Once I have the Heaven's Light in me hands, I will be able to leap through time! The seas of years ago will once again belong to Captain Skunkbeard!"

While the pirates were listening to Captain Skunkbeard's speech, the gang and Skip Jones snuck away. They went through a door to the ship's galley, the kitchen area where the pirates ate. Pots and pans swayed overhead with the movement of the ship.

"Why would Captain Skunkbeard believe he could time-travel?" Velma wondered. "It doesn't make sense."

"If you ask me, that guy is a few doubloons short of a treasure," Shaggy remarked, which made Scooby-Doo laugh. As Scooby chuckled, he slapped the wall, causing a secret door to open!

"*Whoa!*" The gang and Skip Jones all gasped as they entered the room. It was full of high-tech equipment, dials, control panels, and screens. Models of the things they had seen just before were also in the room: the World War I airplanes, the old ship, even the sea monster. A projector of some sort was aimed out the porthole window. "Like, what is all this stuff?" Shaggy asked.

"They look like Captain Skunkbeard's Phantoms of the Bermuda Triangle," Skip Jones said.

"That's exactly what they are," Velma told everyone. "They're remote-control models designed to look full size from a distance when projected as holograms, lifelike 3-D images, through this projector. Someone wants to make sure the Bermuda Triangle looks real."

"But why?" Daphne asked. "Who are they trying to fool? And what's happened to all the passengers?"

"I don't know," Fred admitted. "But all this stuff gives me an idea for a plan."

"That's my boy," Skip Jones said proudly.

Chapter 7

The ghost pirate ship passed through a secret passage into a ring of rocks. The ship was now in the water-filled crater of a huge sunken volcano. Thunder boomed and lightning lit up the sky. Captain Skunkbeard gave a command, and the pirates lowered a large, mechanical claw over the side of the ship and into the water. "Now raise the Heaven's Light from the briny deep!" he shouted to Sea Salt Sally, who was working the claw's control lever.

Rupert stood on deck along with the other pirates. He couldn't believe that the pirates believed they could find a meteor that had fallen to Earth over two hundred years ago!

It took three strong pirates to pull at the crank and raise the claw. After much hard labor, the water around the ship took on a golden glow! Finally, a gigantic meteor came up above the water's surface. The pirates used the claw to gently swing it over the ship's deck.

"I can't believe it!" Rupert gasped.

The pirates cleared a path as Captain Skunkbeard, followed by Wooden Leg Wally and Sea Salt Sally, approached the meteor. Captain Skunkbeard pulled out his sword and plunged it into the meteor. The sword sunk in a few inches and Captain Skunkbeard leaned his weight into the sword, trying to pry open the meteor.

A brilliant golden light shone out of the crack in the meteor's surface!

At the same time, eerie lights began to shine down on the deck of the ship. "Wha — What's happening?" Wooden Leg Wally stammered fearfully.

"It worked!" Captain Skunkbeard shouted. "Time itself has become undone!"

He and his crew shielded their eyes as the strange lights grew brighter and began spinning wildly. Two dark figures stepped out of the bright glare of light — two aliens in sleek silver suits, with large eyes!

"Arrogant humans!" the first alien scolded in

a loud, high-pitched, voice. "You are too small and weak for the power of the Heaven's Light!"

The second figure stepped forward and spoke in the same alien voice. "Return it to the sea! Release your captives — or pay the price!"

A flying saucer swooped down over the ghost ship, blinding everyone with its bright light.

The pirates didn't realize that the aliens were really Fred and Daphne in disguise. Voice scramblers were giving their words an alien sound. And Velma was hidden behind some barrels, operating a remote control to create the holographic image of the space ship.

The last thing the pirates didn't realize as they huddled together in fear was that Scooby and Shaggy were hidden and holding the ends of a net. They were just waiting for a signal from Fred and then they would drop the net over the pirates!

The storm around them was becoming worse. Thunder boomed while lightning crashed. The water around the ship began to bubble and steam. Soon it was boiling! Everyone on board — including the aliens — struggled to stay standing as the boiling water rocked the ship.

The motion of the rocking ship loosened a stack of cannonballs, sending them rolling across the deck. One of them landed right on Scooby-Doo's foot! Hopping in pain, Scooby dropped the end of the net. It dropped to the deck and missed Captain Skunkbeard and his pirates by inches!

"Argh! Methinks something is fishy around here!" Captain Skunkbeard bellowed.

"Don't change the subject, humans," Fred the alien told him. He was starting to panic. His plan wasn't turning out as he'd planned!

Now Captain Skunkbeard understood what had been going on. "So! Trying to spring a trap, are ye!" he accused, glaring angrily at Fred and Daphne.

Fred and Daphne backed away. "Uh . . . we come in peace?" Fred said weakly.

Captain Skunkbeard pointed his sword and ordered his pirate crew to seize them. "*Arrrggghhh!!!*" the pirates yelled as they ran toward Fred and Daphne, swords raised. Daphne and Fred ran. Rupert tried to escape and Velma came out of hiding to try to help, but before long they were all cornered by the pirates.

"Like, yo ho ho!" someone shouted from above.

Everyone looked up.

Shaggy stood in the ship's crow's nest, a dagger between his teeth, a patch over one eye, and a pirate's hat on his head. Scooby-Doo was beside him wearing a pirate's hat, too. Lightning flashed in the sky as Shaggy plunged his dagger into the sail. Scooby jumped on his back and together they slid down the length of the sail on the dagger, pirate-style.

They landed on the deck beside a rowboat that was hanging, suspended from ropes. "Captain Skunkbeard, your jib is up!" Shaggy told him.

Using his dagger, Shaggy sliced some of the ropes holding the rowboat. The rowboat now acted like a huge swing gliding across the deck, scooping up ghost pirates as it went. The motion made all the ship's ropes and pulleys act like a giant mousetrap — one pulling on the other, making it move — until the whole pirate crew, including Captain Skunkbeard, was tossed into the net as it was pulled up once again by the sliding ropes.

"Nice work, guys," Fred told Shaggy and Scooby-Doo.

"But who was behind all this madness?" Rupert asked.

Reaching up to the net where Captain Skunkbeard dangled helplessly, Fred pulled off the pirate's hat and wig.

Chapter 8

"Biff Wellington, of course," Velma said.

"He was after the meteor all this time," Daphne added. "But he needed Rupert to find it."

"But why go to all that trouble for a meteor?" Fred wondered aloud.

Biff Wellington pulled himself up to a sitting position inside the net. "All my life, I was fascinated with pirates," he explained. "I wanted to be a master of the sea. The meteor would give me the power to control the Bermuda Triangle and time travel!"

The gang exchanged confused glances. Why would anyone think such a thing?

"Like, that's nuts!" Shaggy remarked.

"Mr. Wellington, where on Earth did you get such a crazy idea?" Velma asked him.

Wooden Leg Wally stepped forward. "He

got it from me!" he announced. "It was the only way I could get him to pay for a search for the meteor. I convinced him that he had once been a famous pirate in his past life!"

Velma was starting to understand. "So you used remote-control vessels that you projected as holograms to fool Mr. Wellington into believing that the legends of the Bermuda Triangle were true!"

Wooden Leg Wally nodded. "And I'll get away with it, too — *in spite* of you meddling kids!"

"But why do you want a meteor so badly?" Fred asked.

Wooden Leg Wally grinned. "It's not called the Heaven's Light for nothing!" he said. He jammed his sword into the hole Captain Skunkbeard had made and twisted it with all his strength, prying the hole open. The widening crack in the meteor revealed even more of the golden glow. "It's solid gold!" he revealed.

Wooden Leg Wally turned toward Biff Wellington and laughed. "This gold makes me richer than you are, Wellington," he sneered. "No more taking your orders, feeding your fantasies, putting up with your quirky habits. Now I will be the true master of the sea!"

The storm above them became even stronger. The waters around them churned wildly, rocking the ship, as thick clouds of steam rose from the waves.

"Like, I'm getting seasick," Shaggy complained.

"*Ree, roo,*" Scooby agreed, holding his belly.

"Raising the meteor has caused some kind of volcanic activity," Rupert told them all.

Biff Wellington raised his arms dramatically. "It's the Triangle, you fools!" he shouted. "She wants her meteor back!"

"As crazy as that sounds, he's probably right," Fred said. "We've got to dump the rock."

Scooby-Doo hurried to the crane controls, ready to lower the meteor. But Wooden Leg Wally leaped across the deck at him and put a sword to Scooby's throat. He wasn't about to lose his golden meteor.

Shaggy rushed to Scooby's aid. "Like, bad idea, man," he told Wooden Leg Wally as he tried to pull him off Scooby. Wooden Leg Wally held tight, but Scooby-Doo used his tail to tickle Wally's ribs. The greedy fake pirate broke into howls of laughter, dropping his sword and his hold on Scooby-Doo.

Scooby instantly yanked back on the crane's lever, causing the meteor to swing out over the ocean. He released the claw's grip and dropped the giant, gold-filled space rock back into the wildly churning water.

"We've got to get out of here!" Daphne shouted as the ship leaned dangerously to one side, tossed by the violent waves.

Fred grabbed the ship's wheel and sailed it out toward the cave they'd gone through when they entered. As they went, the cave began to crumble. Pieces of rock smashed down around them. Stalactites from the cave's ceiling fell, piercing the upper deck of the ship like spears. Fred's expert driving skills were put to good use as he steered this way and that, dodging falling debris. The moment he brought the ship out into the open water, the entire cave crashed down behind them.

"That was close," Daphne said with a sigh of relief. "Good driving, Fred."

"A guy's gotta do what a guy's gotta do," Fred said modestly. "Now let's find my parents." Letting go of the wheel, he walked to the net full of captured pirates and released it. The phony pirates tumbled out onto the deck.

Scooby-Doo stood guard over Wooden Leg Wally, his tickling tail ready to strike if the pirate tried to get away. The rest of the gang went from pirate to pirate, uncovering their true identities.

"Sunny St. Cloud!" Fred cried, pulling off the first pirate's mask.

The ship's cruise director looked up, but she was sleepy and just curled into a ball. "Let me sleep ten more minutes, Mom," she mumbled groggily.

One by one the gang unmasked the pirates. Captain Crothers and all the cruise passengers had been disguised as pirates. Rupert found his entire crew there. They all appeared dazed and sleepy. Fred searched hard for his parents but didn't see them.

"I can't believe that all these people were involved in this plan to find the meteor," Daphne said.

"They weren't," Velma told her, "at least not consciously."

"Like . . . huh?" asked Shaggy. He had *no* idea what was going on.

"Let's see who the real Wooden Leg Wally is," Velma continued, "and that will explain every-thing!" She walked over to where Scooby-Doo was guarding Wooden Leg Wally. "Scooby, do the honors, please."

Wooden Leg Wally squirmed, trying to avoid Scooby's reach, but Scooby quickly pulled off his mask.

Chapter 9

"Mr. Mysterio!" cried Daphne, Fred, and Shaggy.

"But . . . I don't understand!" Rupert blurted.

"Wooden Leg Wally is really Mr. Mysterio, also know as Wally Wigglesworth, the assistant to Mr. Wellington," Velma explained. "He used his position on the mystery cruise to foster the myth of the Bermuda Triangle in order to keep traffic away from the area while his boss searched for the Heaven's Light meteor."

Mr. Mysterio glared angrily at the gang. "And it was working until you came along," he said with a growl in his voice.

"As part of his act, he hypnotized the passengers on the mystery cruise," Velma went on. "When the fake pirates attacked, he used his power over the passengers and convinced them they were crew members of Captain Skunkbeard's pirate ship."

"But where are my parents?" Fred cried, upset because he still hadn't found them.

Velma was about to say that she didn't know, when something alarming caught her eye. Sea Salt Sally was using her sword to force a blindfolded Skip Jones out onto the ship's plank.

"Jinkies!" Velma shouted, pointing. "Fred, look!"

Everyone turned and saw it, too. Skip Jones was pleading with Sea Salt Sally to let him go but she kept pushing onward, going farther onto the plank and calling him a "treacherous scoundrel."

Velma faced Mr. Mysterio. "Release them from your spell," she demanded.

Scooby wiggled his tail threateningly and Mr. Mysterio knew he had no choice. "Alazamboozle," he shouted.

All the cruise ship's crew members and passengers woke up suddenly. Sea Salt Sally pulled off her mask — beneath it was Mrs. Jones!

"Mom!" Fred cried happily.

Mrs. Jones smiled at him but then noticed her husband out on the plank. "Skip! Come in from out there. You could fall off!"

Skip Jones pulled off his blindfold and stared at his wife in amazement. "Peggy? Is that you?"

The plank wobbled dangerously. Skip and Peggy Jones waved their arms wildly, trying to keep their balance, but they tottered dangerously. Any second they would fall into the ocean!

"Scooby, let's work some magic," Velma suggested.

"*Ralazamboozle!*" Scooby-Doo agreed.

Velma grabbed the remote control from the floor and pressed some buttons. A small fleet of the model World War I planes took to the sky. Velma directed them to swoop down and hook Peggy and Skip Jones on their wings at the very moment the couple was about to totter into the ocean.

The planes carried Fred's parents to safety back on the ship. "Pop! Mom!" Fred cried, wrapping them in hugs.

A little while later, the Joneses, Rupert Garcia,

and the gang were all headed back to dry land. "I've notified the authorities and they'll pick up Biff Wellington and Wally Wigglesworth when we arrive back in Miami," Captain Crothers told them.

"What a trip!" Peggy Jones said. "Wait until your next birthday, Freddie. Would you like a ski trip to the Himalayas?"

"Skiing and Abominable Snowmen!" Shaggy cried in a high, trembling voice. "No, thanks! How about some nice safe cake and ice cream!"

Everyone laughed. They were in good moods and ready to head home. Peggy Jones couldn't wait to get all her pictures developed and put them in her scrapbook.

In the navigation cabin, Captain Crothers let Scooby-Doo take the ship's wheel. While he steered, he saw one of the leftover pirate's hats and swept it up, placing it on his head. "Ro-ho-ho!" he shouted, "Rooby-dooby-doo!"

ANTARCTICA

by Madeline Donaldson

PULL AHEAD BOOKS
Continents

Lerner Publications • Minneapolis

Lerner Publications Company
A division of Lerner Publishing Group, Inc.
241 First Avenue North
Minneapolis, MN 55401 USA

For reading levels and more information, look up this title at www.lernerbooks.com.

Words in **bold type** are explained in a glossary on page 30.

Library of Congress Cataloging-in-Publication Data

Donaldson, Madeline.
    Antarctica / by Madeline Donaldson.
        p.   cm. – (Pull ahead books)
    Summary: Introduces the continent of Antarctica and some of its unique characteristics. Includes bibliographical references and index.
        ISBN-13: 978–0–8225–4724–2 (lib. bdg. : alk. paper)
        ISBN-10: 0–8225–4724–4 (lib. bdg. : alk. paper)
        1. Antarctica—Juvenile literature. [1. Antarctica.] I. Title. II. Series.
    Gu63.D66 2005
    919.8'9–dc21   2003011217

Manufactured in the United States of America
7 – BR – 2/15/16

Photographs are used with the permission of: © Kevin Schafer, pp. 3, 9, 15, 16-17, 19, 25; © Paul Souders/WorldFoto, p. 6; © Keith Robinson/B&C Alexander, p. 7; © Josh Landis/National Science Foundation, pp. 8, 24, 26-27; © Royalty-Free/CORBIS, p. 10; © Tim Davis/CORBIS, p. 11; © Gerald and Buff Corsi/Focus on Nature, Inc., pp. 12, 14, 18, 20; © Paul Drummond/B&C Alexander, p.13; © F. Todd/B&C Alexander, p.21; © Michele Burgess, p. 22; © Eugene Schulz, p. 23. Maps on pp. 4-5 and 29 by Laura Westlund.

Whee! Where could you watch
penguins slide across thick ice?

The **continent** of Antarctica!
A continent is a big piece of land.
There are seven continents on Earth.

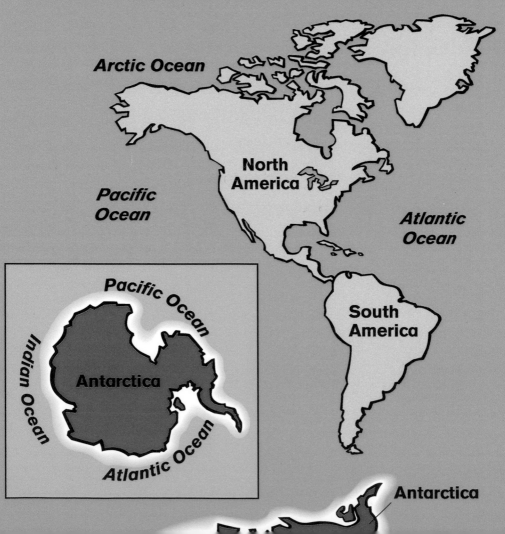

You can find Antarctica on a **globe.** Antarctica is at the bottom. Oceans surround Antarctica.

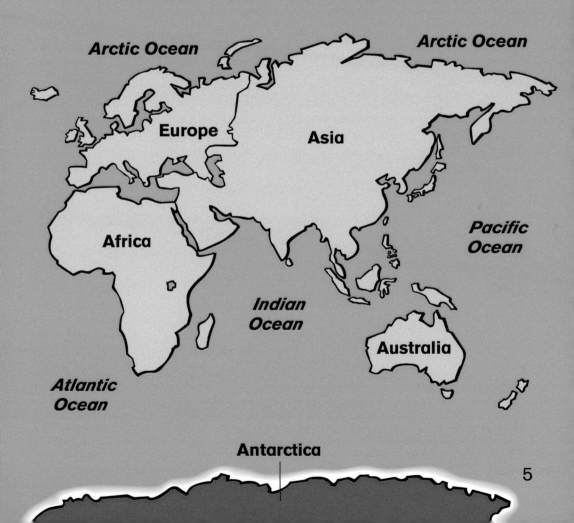

Arctic Ocean

Arctic Ocean

Europe

Asia

Africa

Pacific Ocean

Indian Ocean

Australia

Atlantic Ocean

Antarctica

5

Deep ice and snow cover Antarctica all year long.

Plop, crash! Sometimes a large piece of ice breaks off from Antarctica. The chunks of floating ice are called **icebergs.**

The Transantarctic Mountains cross
the whole continent. They are covered
in thick ice that never goes away.

This very old ice sometimes looks blue.

Antarctica is the coldest place on Earth.
Strong winds blow through Antarctica.

Brrrr! Sometimes the winds blow hard.
Then Antarctica feels even colder.

Not many plants and animals can live in Antarctica. It is too cold.

But this bird,
called a
sheathbill, can
live there.

Seven different kinds of penguins make their homes in Antarctica and on nearby **islands.** These are gentoo penguins.

Chinstrap penguins look like they have
a strap under their chins.

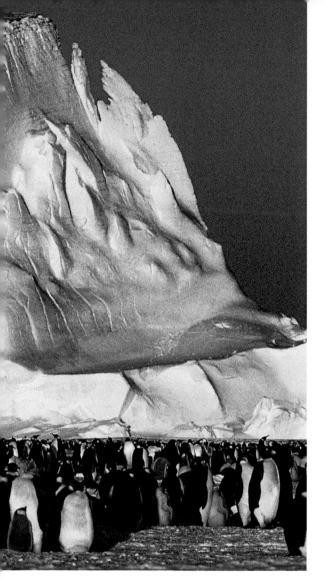

Groups of emperor penguins huddle together. They are warming baby penguins, called **chicks.**

Penguins swim in the cold ocean.
They catch fish for food.

18

The penguins' wings work like flippers.
The flippers help penguins swim fast.

Seals sleep the day away. They keep warm by staying close to one another.

Whales visit Antarctica's waters
in the summer.

This ship is bringing people to visit Antarctica. But no one lives there all the time.

Many **countries** send **scientists** to study Antarctica.

The scientists study the air, the ice, or the wildlife of Antarctica.

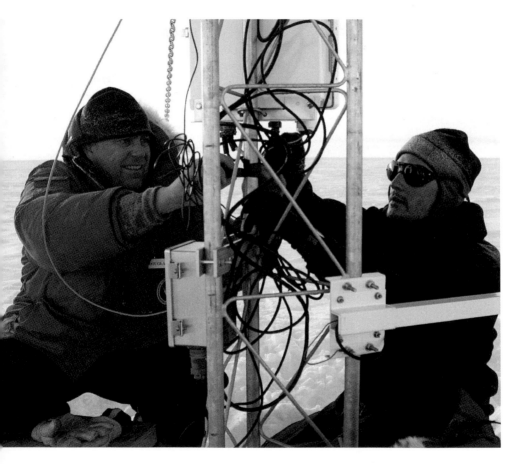

Other people come to Antarctica just
for fun. They must dress warmly.

Do you know about the South Pole? The South Pole is at the very bottom of Earth.

Explorers have traveled there by dogsled, by plane, and on skis.

There's always
something new to
learn about Antarctica!

Cool Facts about Antarctica

- Antarctica covers more than five million square miles (about fourteen million square kilometers).

- The Transantarctic Mountains cut Antarctica into two parts. The parts are called West Antarctica and East Antarctica.

- The Vinson Massif is the highest place on Antarctica. It is in West Antarctica.

- The average temperature on Antarctica is −58 degrees Fahrenheit (−50 degrees Celcius).

- The coldest temperature ever recorded on Antarctica was −128.6 degrees F. (−89.2 degrees C.)

- Winds in Antarctica can reach speeds of up to 200 miles (322 kilometers) per hour.

- The kinds of penguins on and near Antarctica are the emperor, the king, the Adélie, the chinstrap, the gentoo, the macaroni, and the rockhopper.

Map of Antarctica

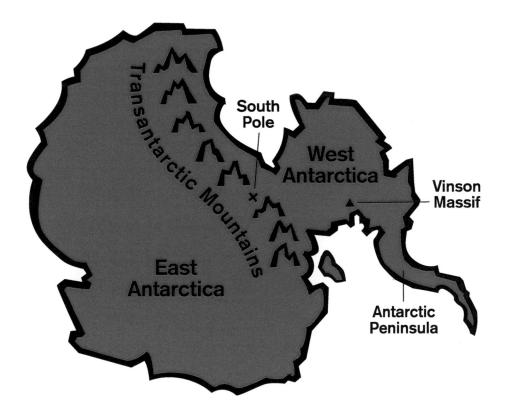

South Pole

Transantarctic Mountains

West Antarctica

Vinson Massif

East Antarctica

Antarctic Peninsula

Glossary

chicks: baby penguins

continent: one of seven big pieces of land on Earth

countries: places with their own governments and borders (or edges)

globe: a ball-shaped Earth that shows the location of countries, continents, oceans, and seas

icebergs: large pieces of ice that have completely broken away from an even larger body of ice

islands: pieces of land surrounded by water

scientists: people who study life on Earth

Further Reading and Websites

Books

Chester, Jonathan. *A Is for Antarctica.* Berkeley, CA: Tricycle Press, 1998.

Foster, Leila Merrell. *Antarctica.* Crystal Lake, IL: Heinemann Library, 2001.

Fowler, Allan. *Antarctica.* Danbury, CT: Children's Press, 2001.

Peterson, David. *Antarctica.* Danbury, CT: Children's Press, 1999.

Pringle, Laurence P. *Antarctica: The Last Unspoiled Continent.* New York: Simon & Schuster, 1992.

Sayre, April Pulley. *Hooray for Antarctica!* Minneapolis: Lerner Publications Company, 2003.

Websites

Enchanted Learning
http://www.enchantedlearning.com/geography/antarctica
The geography section of this website features links to every continent.

InfoPlease
http://www.infoplease.com/atlas/antarctica.html
Search the Antarctica section of this website for history, weather, and science information.

Index